Katie's Picture Show

James Mayhew

A BANTAM LITTLE ROOSTER BOOK™

NEW YORK · TORONTO · LONDON · SYDNEY · AUCKLAND

KATIE'S PICTURE SHOW
A Bantam Little Rooster Book / October 1989

PRINTING HISTORY
Published in Great Britain by Orchard Books in 1989

Little Rooster is a trademark of Bantam Books, a division of
Bantam Doubleday Dell Publishing Group, Inc.

Library of Congress Cataloging-in-Publication Data

Mayhew, James.
  Katie's picture show.
  "A Bantam little rooster book"
  Summary: While visiting the museum with her
grandmother, Katie has a fantastic adventure going
into and becoming part of the pictures she sees.
  [1. Museums—Fiction.   2. Art appreciation—Fiction] I. Title.
PZ7.M4684Kat   1989   [Fic]   89-427
ISBN 0-533-05846-0

Published simultaneously in the United States and Canada

Bantam Books are published by Bantam Books, a division of Bantam
Doubleday Dell Publishing Group, Inc. Its trademark, consisting of
the words "Bantam Books" and the portrayal of a rooster, is
Registered in U.S. Patent and Trademark Office and in other
countries. Marca Registrada. Bantam Books, 666 Fifth Avenue,
New York, New York 10103.

PRINTED IN BELGIUM

Katie and her grandma were in London for the whole day. When it started to rain Grandma said, "Let's go into the museum and look at some pictures."

Katie took Grandma in through a big revolving door (the one marked "No Entry," of course), spinning her around and around at least seven times.

NO ENTRY

Katie had never been to a museum before. "It's wonderful!" she said.

"I need to sit down for a moment after those dreadful doors," gasped Grandma. "You go and look at the pictures, Katie. Be sure to be back in half an hour."

The first few rooms Katie came to were full of people. Katie didn't like crowds, so she went on until she found an empty room.

There were lots of pictures in the room. Katie didn't know which one to look at first. She stopped in front of a painting of a horse-drawn cart.

The Hay Wain *by John Constable,* she read.
PLEASE DO NOT TOUCH.

"Why not?" said Katie, poking a fairly dirty finger at the picture. To her surprise, it went right past the frame and into the painting.

"This isn't a picture at all," cried Katie, astonished. "It's real!" Then, looking carefully around her, she climbed *right into the painting!*

"This is fun!" said Katie. She marched off through the mud toward a cottage. A delicious smell of cooking came from an open window.

Katie found a freshly-baked apple pie cooling on the windowsill. She helped herself to a rather large slice. It was such a good apple pie that she ate the rest, as well.

"Hey, that was my supper," shouted one of the men on the cart. His dog started to bark at Katie, and she thought it would be best to leave. She ran back to the picture frame and climbed down into the museum.

Katie peered around the doorway of the next room. There was a guard sitting next to the door, but he was asleep.

Katie went up to the painting she liked best.
Jean-Auguste-Dominique Ingres, she read. PLEASE DO
NOT TOUCH. But, of course, she did.

"Hello, I'm Katie," said Katie to a lady sitting beside a mirror.

"*Enchantée!*" replied the lady. "I am Madame Moitessier."

"What a lovely dress," said Katie politely. "Are you French?"

"*Mais oui!*" replied Madame Moitessier. "And very lonely. We sit here, being looked at, but no one has ever come inside before. Now, you will stay for some tea, yes?"

"Please," said Katie.

"I have some cream cakes, too. Now, *un* lump or *deux*?" asked Madame Moitessier, pointing to the sugar bowl.

"*Trois!*" said Katie.

So they talked and talked. And they enjoyed themselves, watching the surprised faces of the other visitors to the museum.

"I have not laughed so much for years!" said Madame Moitessier. She was quite overcome. She had to use her fan to calm herself down.

But Katie laughed so much that she spilled her tea (it was her fourth cup) all over Madame Moitessier's dress.

"Oh, you clumsy child!" shrieked Madame Moitessier.

Katie, who had also managed to get mud all over the carpet, decided to leave. She helped herself to another cream cake, climbed out of the picture and back into the museum.

Katie wandered into another room and went
straight up to the biggest picture.

Pierre-Auguste Renoir—**Les Parapluies**, she read.
Katie knew that was French for umbrellas. Then she
noticed a little girl with a hoop in the painting.

I wonder if she'll play with me? she thought.

PLEASE DO NOT TOUCH, said the sign, but, once
again, she did.

"Would you like a cream cake?"
Katie asked the little girl.

"*Merci,*" she replied. "You can
play with my hoop if you like."

Soon they were having quite a
game, bowling the hoop to one
another. All the other people watched
from under their umbrellas.

But Katie hit the hoop too hard, and it flew right out of the picture! It bounced on the floor and disappeared into another painting. The little girl started to cry.

"Whoops!" said Katie. "I'd better try to find it."
She jumped out of the Renoir painting and ran over
to the other picture.

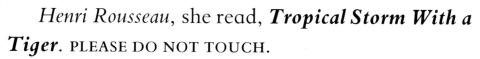

Henri Rousseau, she read, ***Tropical Storm With a Tiger***. PLEASE DO NOT TOUCH.

But Katie couldn't see the hoop, so she climbed over the frame and into the picture.

Katie found herself in a wild jungle. The wind blew, and it was raining very hard. She was rather afraid of the tiger, but he was even more afraid of her. He ran off into the trees.

Katie still couldn't see the hoop, so she wandered off to explore.

Eventually she came to a lake full of crocodiles. They snapped their jaws at her, but Katie just laughed and climbed up a banana tree where they couldn't reach her. She helped herself to a banana.

Just then Katie saw the hoop hanging on a branch. She pulled it down and then found her way back to the picture frame and jumped into the gallery.

Katie threw the hoop back into the Renoir picture.
"Here it is!" she said. The little girl was very
pleased. They waved good-bye to each other, and
Katie ran off into the next room.

Exhibition of Modern Art, read Katie. *All the paintings are lent with kind permission.* DO NOT TOUCH.

Katie looked at a very different picture.

Kasimir Malevich, **Dynamic Suprematism**, she read. It would be fun to climb up that big triangle, she thought.

Without checking to see if anyone was watching, she climbed inside the painting.

When Katie reached the big triangle, she climbed up to the top and slid down the other side.

"Wonderful!" she cried. This was the best picture yet.

But Katie couldn't stop, and she fell farther and farther into the painting. It was like falling into a great big mouth.

"Help!" she cried. She was very scared. She didn't want to be eaten by a piece of modern art.

Katie heard a shout. "Hang on there!" It was the
guard. He threw a rope into the painting. Katie held
on to it with all her strength, and the guard pulled her
back to the picture frame.

"That will teach you to obey signs," he said.

"Sorry," said Katie, who was covered with
splotches of paint. "I don't think I'll ever do that
again."

After she had cleaned herself up (which took quite a while because the splotches of paint were so sticky), Katie thanked the guard and went to find her grandma.

Grandma was snoozing on a comfortable chair.

"You're late," she said when Katie woke her. "I hope you had a nice time."

"Oh, yes!" said Katie. "I really like looking at pictures."

It had stopped raining. So, after Katie had bought postcards of her favorite pictures, they went to find a cup of tea and a cream cake.

Katie's pictures are:

The Hay Wain
by *John Constable* (1776–1837)

Madame Moitessier Seated
by *Jean-Auguste-Dominique Ingres*
(1780–1867)

Les Parapluies
by *Pierre-Auguste Renoir* (1841–1919)

Tropical Storm With a Tiger
by *Henri Rousseau* (1844–1910)

Dynamic Suprematism
by *Kasimir Malevich* (1878–1937)

The first four of Katie's paintings can be found in the National Gallery in London, England, the fifth in the Tate Gallery, also in London. Other paintings by these artists can be found in major museums in the United States and Canada, as well.

As Katie discovered, museums are full of wonderful paintings to enjoy. If you can't visit London to see the real paintings in this book, there is sure to be a museum or gallery near you where there are other interesting pictures to see. Many of them will have a special children's tour.

Although in the story Katie did touch the paintings, you must not. This is because the paintings are all very precious and could easily be damaged.

Don't try to look at too many paintings on one visit—just choose a few, as Katie did, and look at all the detail, shapes, and colors.

All artists have a different way of seeing the world around them. If you paint a picture, it won't look anything like the one a friend might paint. James Mayhew painted the pictures of Katie and her adventures, and you will see that these pictures look different than the five paintings Katie climbed into.

So, when you visit an art museum, look closely at the paintings and see how much you can find out about the way each artist paints.